Published in the United States 2011 by

🍎 Blue Apple Books

515 Valley Street, Maplewood, NJ 07040

www.blueapplebooks.com

First Edition
Printed in China 07/11
HC ISBN: 978-1-60905-092-4
2 4 6 8 10 9 7 5 3 1
PB ISBN: 978-1-60905-182-2
2 4 6 8 10 9 7 5 3 1

A day in the office of

Doctor Bugspit

by Elise Gravel

Say "aaah."

BLUE APPLE BOOKS

Doctor Bugspit's outer-space clinic!
DR
BUGSPIT
Flying Saucers
Three-eyed monster's ENTRANCE
EMERGENCY
ENTER AT YOUR OWN RISK!

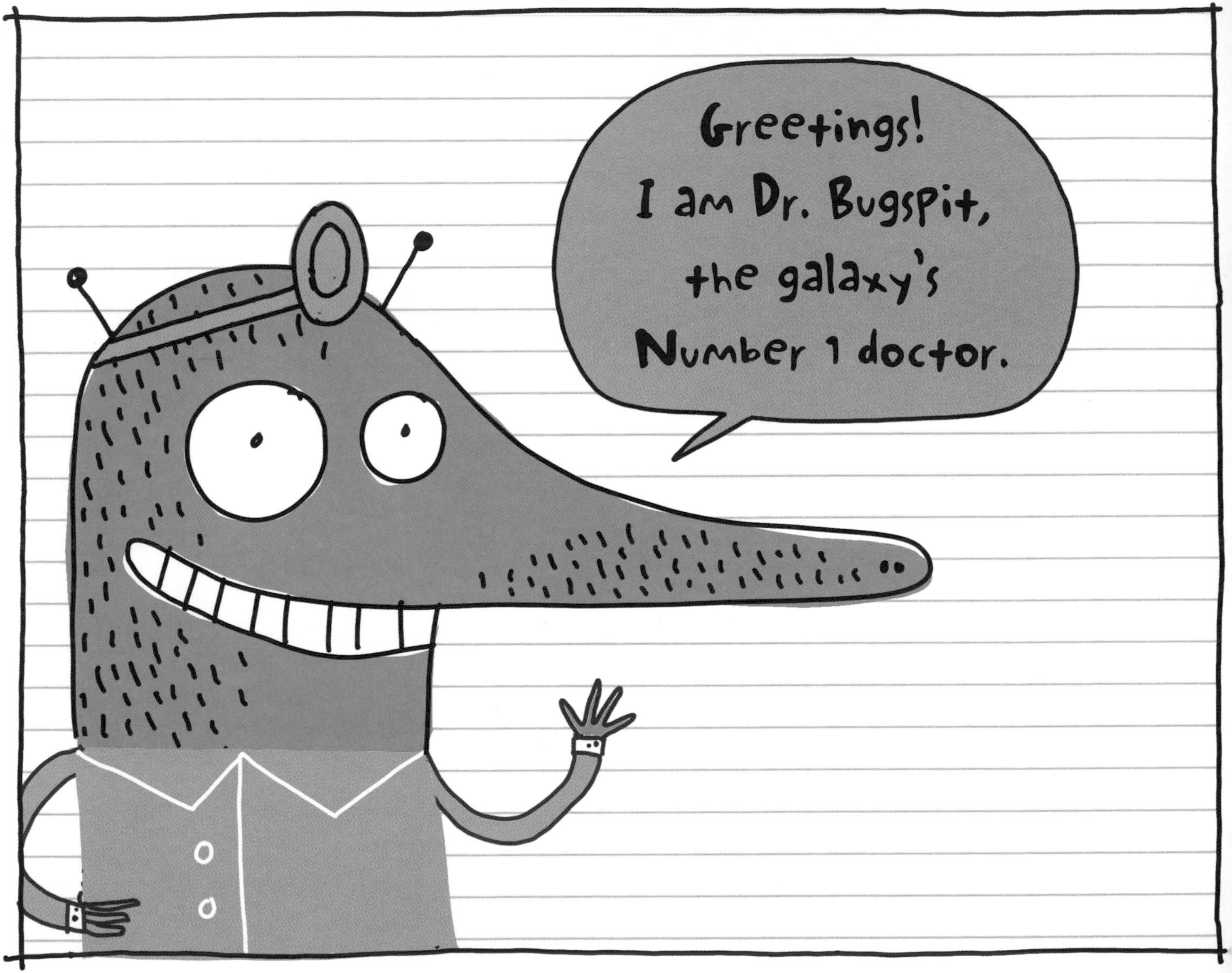
Greetings! I am Dr. Bugspit, the galaxy's Number 1 doctor.

Say hello to Nurse Giggles.
RECEPTION DESK
Wipe your tentacles
HERE

Here's my assistant,
Googoo.
He knows everything
about staying healthy.
Eating lightbulbs
is not a
bright idea.

Creatures from all over come to me for help.

Translation:
GLX = My eye won't blink.

Translation:
PLWZZ = My neck feels strange.

Translation:
OOOOLP = I can't find my mouth!

Doctor Bugspit's
fix-it-up
syrup
Secret ingredients:
SHHH... IT'S A
SECRET.

Nurse Giggles makes the tastiest FLY JAM in the galaxy.
Ingredients:
• fly paste
• fly juice
• fly wings
• fly powder
• artificial fly flavor

DR. BUGSPIT'S EXERCISE BREAK

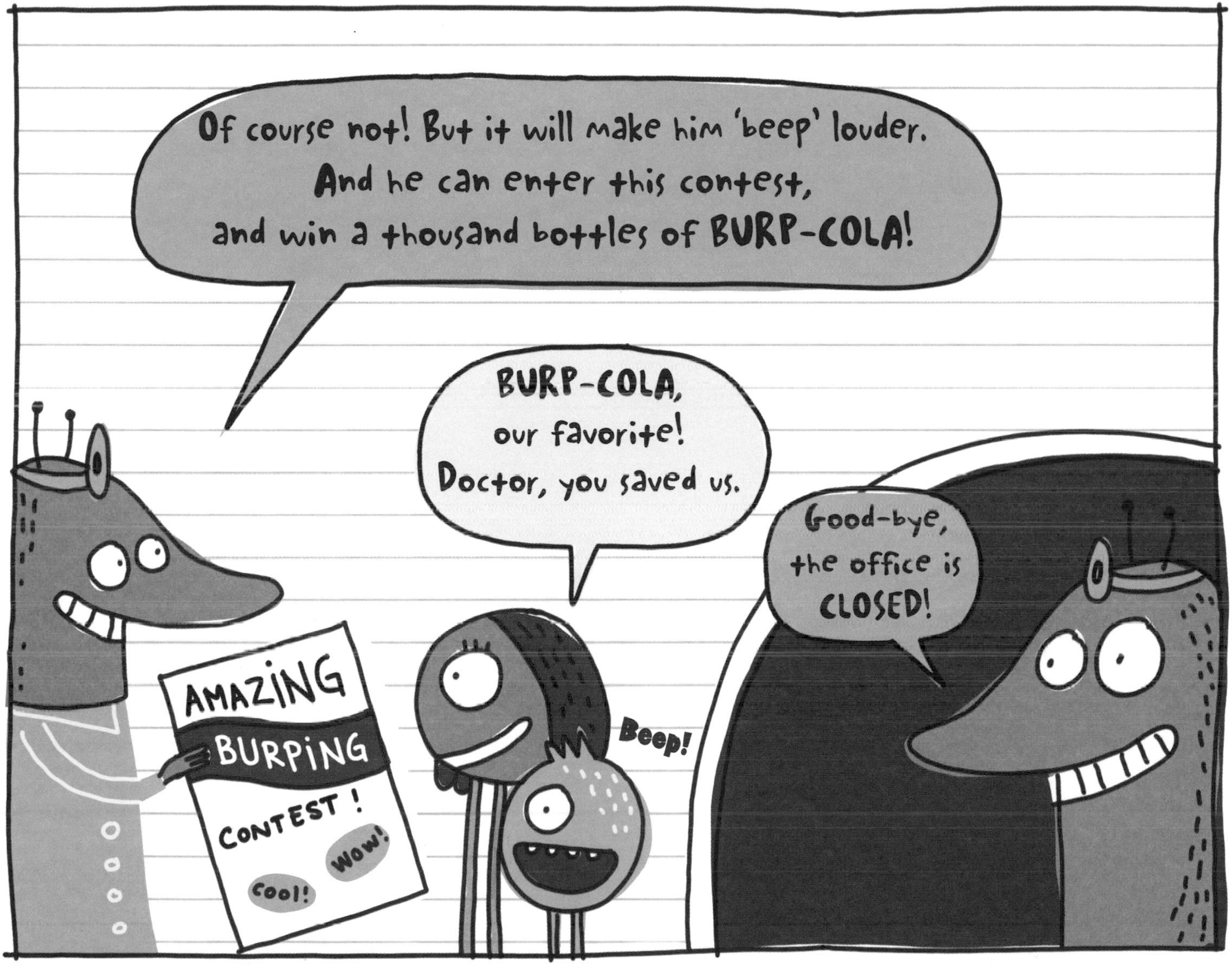
Of course not! But it will make him 'beep' louder. And he can enter this contest, and win a thousand bottles of BURP-COLA!
AMAZING BURPING CONTEST!
Cool!
Wow!
BURP-COLA, our favorite! Doctor, you saved us.
Beep!
Good-bye, the office is CLOSED!

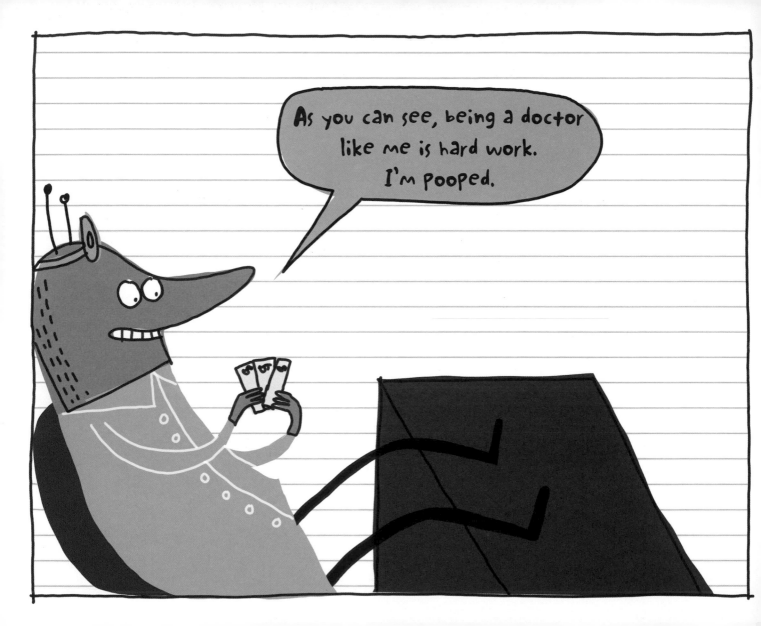

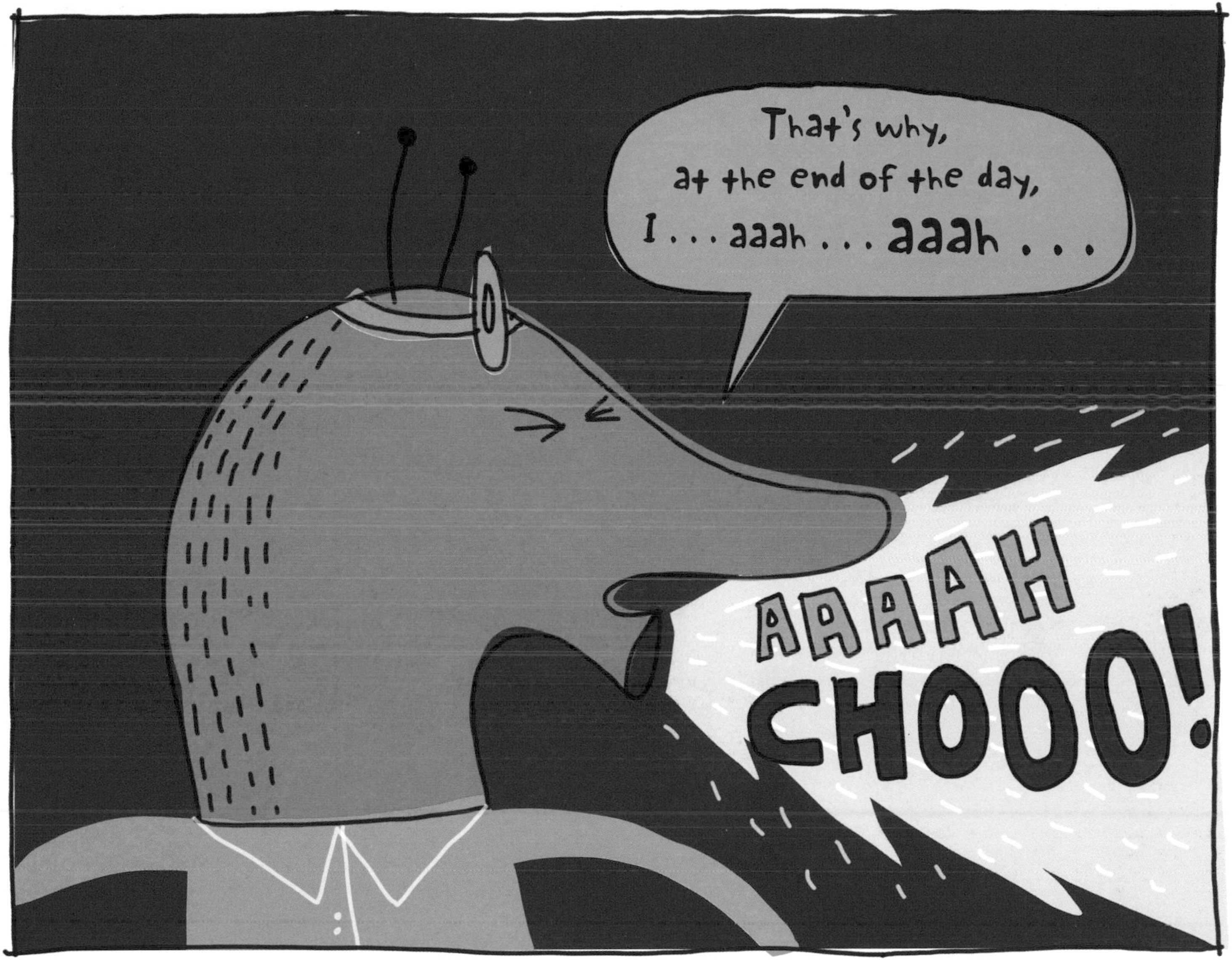
That's why,
at the end of the day,
I . . . aaah . . . aaah . . .
AAAAH
CHOOO!

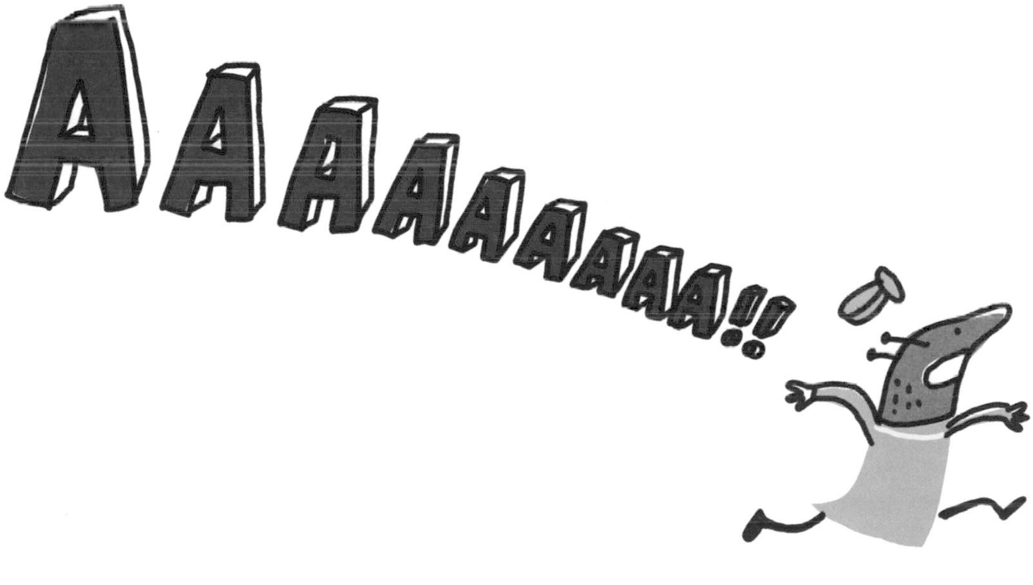
AAAAAAAAA!!